Poppy and

For Georgia
SG

For Nicola
LG

Reading Consultant: Prue Goodwin,
lecturer in education at the University of Reading

ORCHARD BOOKS
338 Euston Road, London NW1 3BH
Orchard Books Australia
Level 17/207 Kent Street, Sydney, NSW 2000
ISBN: 978 1 84362 520 9 (hardback)
ISBN: 978 1 84362 395 3 (paperback)
First published in hardback in Great Britain in 2007
First paperback publication in 2008
Poppy and Max characters © Lindsey Gardiner 2001
Text © Sally Grindley 2007
Illustrations © Lindsey Gardiner 2007

1 3 5 7 9 10 8 6 4 2 (hardback)
1 3 5 7 9 10 8 6 4 2 (paperback)
Printed in Italy by LegoPrint

Orchard Books is a division of Hachette Children's Books,
an Hachette Livre UK company
www.orchardbooks.co.uk

Poppy and Max and the River Picnic

Sally Grindley 🦴 Lindsey Gardiner

ORCHARD BOOKS

One morning, Poppy threw back the curtains and said, "It's a beautiful day, Max. Let's go for a long walk down to the river."

Max opened an eye. "I am not a dog who likes long walks," he said, "unless there is a picnic at the end of them."

Brilliant idea.

"I love picnics!" Poppy cried.

"What shall we take to eat?"
asked Poppy.
"Muffins," said Max. "I love muffins."

"I'll make some sandwiches too,"
said Poppy.

They set off towards the river.
"Let's stop here," said Max when they
reached a bench.

"We've only gone a little
way," said Poppy.
"It seemed a long way to me,"
protested Max.

They walked a little further and came
to a grassy bank.
"Let's have a muffin," said Max.

"We've only just had breakfast,"
cried Poppy.
"Walking makes me hungry,"
grumbled Max.

They walked a little further and
came to a wood.
"This is a good place for a picnic,"
said Max. "I'm stopping here."

"All right, Max," Poppy sighed.
"Let's sit here for a snack, but then
we'll go on with our walk."

Max pulled a muffin out of the
picnic basket.
He was about to bite into it when
Poppy screamed and jumped up.

12

"There are ants everywhere, Max,"
she cried.
"Ants are all right," said Max.

Not in my shorts!

"We'll have to go somewhere else,"
Poppy said.

They walked a little further and came
to a field.
Max sniffed the grass. "This field
is made for picnics. No ants here,"
he said.

Poppy looked. "But there are nettles everywhere, Max."
"Nettles are all right," said Max.

"We'll have to find somewhere else," said Poppy.

They came to another field.
"There are no nettles here," said Max.
"There are no ants either. This is the
perfect place for our picnic."

He sat down and pulled a muffin
from the basket.
"We still can't see the river," said
Poppy sadly. "I wanted to paddle."

"I am not a dog who likes to get his
feet wet," said Max. "Have a muffin."

Max lay back and closed his eyes.

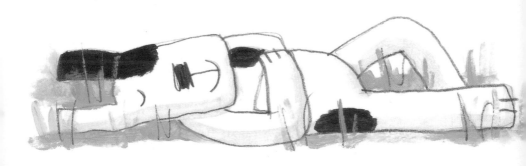

Poppy lay back and looked up at the blue sky.

"I love it when the sun is shining," she
said. "It makes me feel all happy."

"It makes me feel all sleepy,"
muttered Max.

Suddenly, a shadow fell across Poppy.
Another fell across Max.
Poppy sat up and came face to
face with . . . two great, big cows.

Poppy shook Max's paw. "Max, we've got company."

"Send them away," Max muttered. "We're not sharing our picnic."

Then Max opened his eyes and saw the cows. Max leapt to his feet, ran across the field, and away down the path.

When Poppy caught up with him,
Max was sitting in the river.

"Have they gone?" he asked. "I am
not a dog who likes cows."
"Cows are all right," said Poppy.
"What's the water like?"

"Well, it's better than a bath,"
Max said.
Poppy paddled over to him.

"It's lovely and warm," she said,
splashing Max.
Max splashed Poppy back.

Then they splashed and splashed each other until they were dripping wet.

"I'm a soggy doggy," said Max, rolling
in the grass.

"Shall we finish our picnic now?"
asked Poppy.
"About time too," said Max.

They sat by the edge of the river and
ate everything up.

"This has been a brilliant day," smiled Poppy, as they packed up the picnic basket.

"Thank you, Poppy. I am a dog
who likes long walks, after
all," said Max.

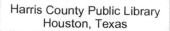

Sally Grindley
Illustrated by Lindsey Gardiner

Poppy and Max are available from all good bookshops,
or can be ordered direct from the publisher:
Orchard Books, PO BOX 29, Douglas IM99 1BQ
Credit card orders please telephone 01624 836000 or fax 01624 837033
or e-mail: bookshop@enterprise.net for details.

To order please quote title, author and ISBN and your full name and address.
Cheques and postal orders should be made payable to 'Bookpost plc'.
Postage and packing is FREE within the UK
(overseas customers should add £1.00 per book).

Prices and availability are subject to change.